THE
SILVER CRANE

THE SILVER CRANE

BY BETTY JEAN LIFTON

Illustrations by Laszlo Kubinyi

THE SEABURY PRESS   NEW YORK

J

L

for
Ruth Hill Viguers—
   in flight

❧Contents

THE
SILVER CRANE

1
The Pond

It was the kind of spring day that any sailor would take to sea. Waga, being a Pekin duck, set out on his own little pond. He let the soft breeze blow him like a kite across the water.

"Never cared much for the ocean or lakes," said Waga, although he had never known them. "Give me my own little pond, snug and secure."

"Me too," said his wife, Hannah, swimming along just behind him.

"I wouldn't trade our quiet little home here for all the fish in the world," continued Waga, puffing his white chest out contentedly.

"Neither would I," said Hannah obediently.

Hannah was a very devoted duck wife and she tried to agree with everything Waga said. This wasn't difficult, since he usually said the same thing every day. But this morning she found it hard to pay attention, for she had just laid her first egg. Yes, her very first one. She could think of nothing but how she would break the news to Waga that there would be ducklings.

Waga did not like surprises. He might not even like ducklings. She must be careful not to startle him. When he was startled he always declared that his day was ruined. He would refuse to go into the feeding pen for his late afternoon snack of cracked corn which the

Master always left there. And after that he could never sleep at night because his stomach was too empty. Oh, it would take all of Hannah's skill to inform Waga in just the right way.

For the past few days Hannah had been slipping off to prepare her nest while Waga was fishing or dozing. She had chosen a spot just in front of the tool shed, in the meadow between the main house and the pond. She had considered the willow tree, on the far side of the pond, but sometimes the Master came by with his lawn mower when she was napping and almost scared her out of her wits. And certainly she would not go near the stone wall that bordered the meadow, although it was the shadiest nook, for just beyond it was the forest where the weasel lived.

Waga did not like to talk about the weasel.

Once during the winter, when the trees had lost their leaves and you could see deep into the woods, Hannah was sure she had seen his long catlike body darting by.

"Waga, I saw the weasel!" she had cried. "He was all white, just like us."

"Nonsense," Waga had said. "Weasels are brown."

"Not in winter." Hannah had persisted. "Their bodies turn white to look like the snow. I know it was a weasel I saw going by."

"Have it your way," said Waga. "I prefer to think of other things, like this fish I'm after right now."

But Hannah could not help brooding about the weasel. Just the night before, an unusually still one, she was certain she could hear the breathing of the small wild animals lying nervously in half sleep beyond the stone wall. It was as if their breaths, rising and falling together, formed a song—as if they were trying to tell her something.

THE SONG OF THE
FOREST ANIMALS

Deep in the woods the weasel lies,
And watches us with evil eyes.
Deep in the woods the weasel waits,
One move from him decides our fates.
Breathe softly as he passes by,
Hide quickly to escape his eye.
Beware the weasel, oh beware!
The weasel watches everywhere.

Of course, she didn't tell Waga. He would call her foolish and insist, as he always did, that the weasel would never come over the wall. No, instead she had decided to tell him this very morning about the ducklings.

"My dear," she began as they were swimming along.

"Don't bother me now," grunted Waga. "I've spotted a fish! There it goes—oops!" And all she could see of him was a tail where his beak had been only a moment before.

Soon he was back up, his stomach distended a little, and they continued on across the placid water of the pond.

"My dear . . . my dear . . ."

"For heaven's sake, Hannah, speak up. Don't just keep repeating 'my dear, my dear.'"

"Yes, my dear . . . I mean, no, my dear! Oh dear, I don't know what I mean!" cried Hannah, all flustered.

"Now don't get excited," said Waga. "You know I hate excitement."

"Well," said Hannah, "I was thinking it is a little lonely here on the pond and—"

"Lonely!" exploded Waga. "This pond is perfect just as it is with the two of us. I will never allow anyone else on it. Don't you remember that only yesterday I had to chase that impossible wild mallard away?"

"I didn't mean *him*, my dear."

"Then who did you mean?"

"Oh, nobody in particular," said Hannah, for at that very moment she caught a glimpse of the same wild mallard coming toward them in the sky.

So that Waga should not become upset again, she added quickly, "You know, my dear, I didn't think that mallard was so bad.

He only asked to stay with us for a few days."

"The nerve!" cried Waga heatedly. "We don't know who he is, or where he comes from."

"He said he is a wandering poet," replied Hannah cautiously.

"And he's got a green head besides!" continued Waga.

"Does it really matter—the color, I mean?" asked Hannah.

"I could never trust anyone with a green head," said Waga firmly, shaking his own white one at her as if to prove his point.

"But he has such a pretty name—Green Hood," said Hannah softly.

"A green-hooded scoundrel, that's what he is!" grunted Waga. "He'd better not come back here again or—" His words were interrupted by a bold, carefree voice singing from the far side of the pond:

THE SONG OF GREEN HOOD

A wandering poet I,
Writing on the sky
From a whirring, blurring height.
My song is free
As the rest of me,
And so shall it be
  Until I go out on my final flight
    Into the dark and duckless night!
    Into the dark and duckless night!
  Until I go out on my final flight.

A wandering lover I,
With a roving eye
For ponds where ducks delight.

 20

To love I sing,

Love on the wing,

So beloved, let me cling,

> *Until I go out on my final flight*
>
> *Into the dark and duckless night!*
>
> *Into the dark and duckless night!*
>
> *Until I go out on my final flight.*

"How beautiful!" sighed Hannah when the song had ended.

But Waga felt otherwise. "It's that green-hooded scalawag again!" he cried, spotting the mallard on the pond. "I'll teach him not to barge in uninvited like this. I'll send him out on his final flight!"

And Waga, stiffening his body and lowering his head like a battering ram, steamed toward him.

2
Green Hood

The poet with the green head watched Waga advancing, but he did not stir from his spot. He was a true wanderer, and knew how to handle a small-pond duck like this one. Or at least he thought he did.

When Waga was practically upon him, Green Hood flapped his wings in greeting and called out cheerily: "Snails and quails, what's the hurry? There's no reason for this flurry!"

"And there's no reason for you to be on my pond again," puffed Waga.

"I told you yesterday I am a poet traveling in search of new songs."

"The best traveler stays at home," retorted Waga.

"Not the best poet," replied the mallard.

"I wouldn't fly even if I could," said Waga. For in truth, Pekin ducks, for all their whiteness, cannot fly.

"A bird *should* fly, or what's a bird for?" said Green Hood brightly. "When spring comes, I feel the urge to soar north and visit ponds very much like this one. And in the winter, I am off again south to compose new poems to the sun."

"Ugh," said Waga with a shudder. "You should be making a permanent home for yourself instead of singing meaningless poems."

"Friend," said Green Hood gravely, "there is no such thing as a permanent home or a meaningless poem."

"My home is permanent, and I intend to keep it that way!" cried Waga. "It is mine, and mine alone."

"I can understand your love for this delightful pond," said Green Hood, the lilt returning to his voice. "Never, in all my travels, have I seen one to compare with it."

"Is that a fact?" said Waga, in spite of himself.

"It is," said Green Hood. "Where else could you flip your feet without fear of snapping turtles? Where else would the fish jump with joy down your gullet?"

"I always suspected it was most unusual," agreed Waga.

"Where else," continued Green Hood con-

fidently, "could you find corn cracked to per-
fection?"

"You'll not touch my corn!" cried Waga,
flying into a rage again as he realized he was
being tricked by this honey-beaked poet. Once
more, like yesterday, he lowered his head for
attack. Once more he charged toward Green
Hood.

Of course it would have been easy for the
mallard to fly off as he had the day before, but
this time Green Hood seemed determined to
stay. At first he just skimmed playfully along
the surface of the water, letting Waga pursue
him at top speed. Occasionally he had to rise
a few feet into the air to keep out of reach of
Waga's angry beak.

The chase was not only on the pond, but
across the meadow too. Yellow feet padded

frantically through the lilac and honeysuckle bushes, around the tool shed (they were racing too fast to notice Hannah's egg) and up to the stone wall.

"Got you!" cried Waga fiercely.

But instead of rising into the air to escape, the poet with the green head did an amazing thing. He stopped so abruptly where he was that Waga almost collided into him. They stood there beak to beak, staring at each other.

"Snails and quails, you win! I give up! I give in!" said Green Hood. And in a hushed voice, as if he were confiding some great secret, he added, "But there is something I must tell you."

"What is it?" demanded Waga suspiciously. He was not going to be tricked by Green Hood again.

"The *real* reason I am here," said Green Hood meekly.

"It had better be good," quacked Waga.

"Oh, what reason?" asked Hannah eagerly, as she caught up with them by the wall.

"I have come here not only in search of new poems," said Green Hood slowly. "I'm searching for something else as well."

"For what?" exclaimed Hannah before Waga could signal her to be silent.

"The Silver Crane."

"The Silver Crane? Never heard of him," grunted Waga.

"You will. All ducks do sooner or later."

"But who is he?" asked Hannah, her heart fluttering with excitement.

"That is a good question," said Green Hood. "No one really knows. He's like a silver ghost, appearing when you least expect him, and disappearing before you can reach him."

"Is he real?" asked Hannah.

"Who can say what is real?" replied the poet. "Some believe he is only a dream. Others that he is just a silver shadow cast on the water when the moon is covered with mist."

"And you—what do you believe?" asked Hannah, ignoring the looks that Waga was giving her.

"I believe that he is real. And that someday I shall see him with my own eyes. Only a few ducks have ever had this experience, and they could hardly speak of it. But they seemed somehow nobler, and more peaceful, after that."

"I doubt if such a bird exists," snorted Waga, for lack of something better to say.

"Perhaps not, perhaps so," said the wild duck—and he did seem sincere now. "But I have dedicated my life to searching for him."

"Well, your Silver Crane is not here," said Waga sharply. "So you can go now."

"I have heard he was heading in this direction," said Green Hood. "Please let me wait here to see if he comes."

"Impossible!" said Waga, his temper rising.

"Just one day," pleaded Green Hood.

"Not one minute," cried Waga, certain now that he was being tricked once more. Again he lowered his head for attack, but this time Green Hood simply rose up into the air over the wall.

"You've a heart like a sour berry," Green Hood called as he disappeared into the forest. "Sour Berry! Sour Berry!"

And after that there was silence.

"Oh dear, what will happen to him in the forest?" wailed Hannah.

"I couldn't care less," grunted Waga. "Calling me a sour berry! The nerve of him!"

"The weasel might get him," moaned Hannah.

"Let the Silver Crane save him," said Waga. "If he exists." But seeing how worried Hannah was, he added, "Green Hood likes danger. He'll manage somehow."

"Oh, I do hope so," sighed Hannah, following him back to shore. "I wouldn't have minded him staying for a few days."

But Waga's dark look made her change the subject. "Come, my dear, rest over by my rock," she suggested. "You must be tired after such a busy chase."

She led him over to her favorite rock on

the bank. It was a magnificent boulder, as smooth and clear as the pond itself. "It might have been a shooting star," Hannah always said. She truly believed it had some magical power if one stayed close to it.

Waga thought Hannah was being silly about this rock, but he didn't mind settling his over-stuffed body near it for a quick snooze. He ached all over from his unaccustomed exercise.

"Now things will return to what they've always been," he told Hannah. "Sour berry, indeed. Hmmmmph!"

But can things always stay the same—don't they have to change just a little? thought Hannah after Waga was breathing heavily in sleep. Green Hood had been like a sweet wind passing through her small world. She liked the way his dapper white collar sat just below his green hood. It went so well with his brown vest and black and white tail. And it pleased her to know there was such a bird as the Silver Crane.

Wouldn't it be wonderful if the Silver Crane really did appear on this pond, mused Hannah. She hoped it would be some misty night after her eggs had hatched so that she and her ducklings-to-be might see him together.

3
Belle

For the next week all was quiet on the pond. Green Hood stayed in the forest. "Wild things do well in wild places," muttered Waga, the one time Hannah dared to wonder aloud how he was faring.

In fact, Waga was doing quite well himself now. He went back to his usual routine of fishing and sleeping and preening himself in the sun. "I guess I got rid of that mallard, all right," he would chuckle occasionally before drifting off to sleep. He didn't even notice that Hannah was having a private life of her own.

Hannah had already laid nine eggs. They lay gleaming white in the nest she had put together from bits of grass and leaves mixed with the soft feathers of her breast. *Her* eggs. She had created them. Her heart beat as joyfully as if they were already little balls of golden feathers chirping up at her. But she hated keeping a secret from Waga. She simply must break the news this very morning now that he was in a good mood again.

"My dear, I've something to tell you," she whispered after waddling down to his side.

"You saw some new fish in the pond," said Waga hopefully.

"No, not that."

"You found another shady spot for nap-ping?"

"No, but do guess again. This is fun."

"Just once more," said Waga, trying to humor her. "You've been up at the big house watching the Master in the garden."

"Don't be silly," giggled Hannah nervously. "You know I am not that brave around the Master."

"You need never be afraid of him," said Waga. "He's only human. And without his cracked corn we'd have to forage for ourselves in the wilderness."

"Like that mallard?"

"Don't mention that green-hooded monster to me," cried Waga. "I'm trying to forget him!"

"Now don't get upset again," said Hannah. "It was just that he liked our cracked corn and I—"

"You what?"

"I'm glad we have the cracked corn, since there'll be little beaks to feed."

"Little beaks? What do you mean? Good heavens, Hannah, you don't mean to say . . . ?"

"I do."

For a few seconds Waga was speechless. Although he usually had an opinion about everything—an opinion he tried never to change—he never expected, of all things, ducklings!

"Gosh!" he finally exclaimed, a word he had not used since he and Hannah were ducklings on the pond together.

"Then you don't mind?" sighed Hannah with relief.

"Mind?" said Waga. "I suppose not. Though you should have told me sooner. I hate surprises."

"I have the loveliest nest with nine eggs. Would you like to see it?"

"Some other time," said Waga. Nests did not really interest him. "But you run along and take care of it as best you see fit," he added more gently.

For the rest of the day Waga felt a strange kind of tingling inside. Life was, after all, good. There would be nine little ducklings on his pond. *His* ducklings. He would teach them how to swim, how to stick their little beaks into the water and poke their tails up into the air to find fish beneath the surface. He would lead them into the feeding pen for their cracked corn. All nine of them would follow obediently after him. They would—and he puffed his white chest out—be all white, just like him. And like Hannah too. Oh, it was too wondrous to even think about.

Just before sundown, Hannah reappeared again.

"My dear, I'll be leaving you alone from now on," she said. "I've got to set for a month on my nest."

"You mean I won't see you at all?"

"I'll be able to stop by for a short while in the late afternoons to have a bite to eat and a swim."

"Well, don't worry about a thing. I'll be all right," Waga reassured her bravely. "Do what you must for our future ducklings."

However, for the next few days with Hannah away on her nest, Waga was very lonely. He looked forward to that brief period every afternoon when she came waddling down to exchange the news. "It was really hot sitting in the sun today," she would say. Or, "I felt a cool breeze at midnight." And he would inform her, "I caught two fish at dawn," or "I had a nice midmorning nap."

However, one afternoon they barely had time to say a word when something unexpected happened. Waga, who hated the unexpected second only to surprises, could only gasp in disbelief. There was his Master walking toward them with something in his arms. It wasn't a bag of corn. It was a *duck*.

"What's going on here?" quacked Waga indignantly.

"Now, Waga, I know that you don't like other birds on the pond, but this is a special case," said his Master firmly, setting the duck down on the bank as he spoke. "Belle, here, and her husband, Captain Splash, were attacked by a weasel yesterday on my friend's pond. She got away but the Captain is still in the hospital with a broken wing. I suggested she wait here where it's safe until he gets out."

"Impossible! I won't allow it!" quacked Waga furiously.

"I hope that you and Hannah will be very kind to Belle and make her feel at home," his Master went right on over his protests. "She's a Muscovy, a slightly different breed from you, but it shouldn't make any difference."

Then he slipped them a few pieces of bread, and if Waga hadn't been so busy gobbling them down, he might have continued objecting. When he finally looked up, the last crumb having been carefully savored, his Master was already walking back to the house as if everything was settled.

Belle sat forlornly on the bank, not even bothering to look at them. Her feathers were all matted and caked, as if she had been through some terrible ordeal.

"What an odd-looking duck," Waga muttered to Hannah. "Her head and neck are white, but her body looks as if someone dumped black and purple paint over her."

"And she has a spot of black on the tip of her beak," whispered Hannah. "And red markings like a mask around her eyes. But, poor dear, she can't help what she looks like."

"I'll chase her away, that's what I'll do,"

fumed Waga. But deep in his heart he knew that his Master meant her to stay. She was not just passing through like a wild duck.

"We should speak to her," said Hannah sympathetically. "She looks so lonely. And imagine being attacked by a weasel. It's too terrible."

"It is a shame," said Waga. "Still we can't take on all the troubles in the world."

It wasn't that Waga meant to be heartless. It was just that he had a certain plan for his life with Hannah and the ducklings on the pond, and it did not include this red-masked Muscovy duck or her husband, should he ever appear.

"But we must say something," insisted Hannah.

"Not a word!" retorted Waga. And then he

had what he considered a brilliant idea. "We'll just pretend she isn't here."

Hannah didn't think this so brilliant, but she knew better than to say so. For the rest of the time she had left on the pond, she swam dutifully after Waga. Belle, as if lost in her own thoughts, seemed not to notice them.

The next afternoon when she left her nest, Hannah saw that Belle had moved under the willow tree. Since Waga was busy chasing a minnow, she swam quickly over to her.

"Are you all right?" she called as she came close.

Belle looked up slowly from behind her red mask. "At least it's quiet," she replied.

"Waga likes it that way," said Hannah, a little shyly.

"Captain Splash liked to have lots of ducks dropping by," said Belle. "We were always laughing and singing together."

"We had a mallard here a few days ago," said Hannah, trying to make her pond sound more interesting. "He was a poet and he had a green head."

"All male mallards have green heads."

"But not all poets, do they?"

"No, I suppose not," replied Belle patiently. And then her eyes flickered for a moment. "Did that . . . that poet mention anything about the Silver Crane?"

"Yes, he did!" said Hannah excitedly. "He was going in search of him."

"And where did he go?" asked Belle, trying to sound casual.

"Over the wall into the woods," said Hannah, not adding that Waga had chased him there. "Why do you ask?"

"No reason," replied Belle abruptly, as if she wished to end the subject.

"I . . . I hope Captain Splash is going to be all right," said Hannah, after a brief pause. "I like his name."

"He's a splasher, that's for sure," said Belle, brightening up for the first time. "He could make more waves on our pond than the motor boat. That is, he could before . . . before . . ." A short, choking sound that seemed a cross between a quack and a cough came from her throat.

"Oh, don't say anything more!" cried Hannah. She was so shaken by the very thought of what had happened to poor Captain Splash that she fairly flew back to her nest, as if a weasel were in pursuit of her. She plopped breathlessly on her nine eggs, her heart pounding, her eyes bulging.

"Dreadful, just dreadful!" she quacked over and over again. But gradually her calm returned as she felt the eggs warm and cosy under her, and remembered that Waga had said the weasel would never come over the wall.

4
Over the Wall

Because he had nothing else to do, Waga began watching Belle out of the corner of his
eye. He did wish she would tidy herself up a
bit. His Hannah was always neatly preened
and feathered. There was certainly enough
water in the pond for bathing. But even when
Belle swam out a way to fish, he noticed that
she merely dipped under and returned to shore
as soon as she had eaten, as if she didn't care

how she looked. And she had such a queer way of moving: thrusting her head out before her and then jerking it back as if she were rowing through the air with it.

"There is no accounting for the behavior of others," Waga told himself. The more he saw of the outside world, the more he disapproved of it.

However, Waga's vow not to speak to Belle was broken when he saw her entering the feeding pen for the first time.

"Not my corn!" he quacked, zooming over.

Belle gave him a long hard stare from behind her red mask, but she didn't say anything. She merely retired to her spot under the willow tree.

"I guess that fixed her," Waga told himself proudly. "She'll not do that again."

She didn't. Instead Belle began wandering about the meadow, poking here and there for odd bits of grass and roots. Then she wandered as far as the tool shed and glanced at Hannah who was setting with her eyes closed on the nest. She paused for a moment, as if this maternal scene stirred something within her, but continued out through the back lawn, past the dark hemlocks and swaying birches to the stone wall. With a flying leap, for Muscovies can fly, she was on top of it.

"Oh, my dear, don't do that!" called Hannah, opening her eyes and spotting Belle in that dangerous position. "There's a weasel over there."

But Belle merely looked into space as if she had heard nothing. Then she casually opened her long wings and lifted off over the treetops and into the forest.

It wasn't that Belle was being brave. It was just that she was certain that the mallard poet Hannah had mentioned must be Green Hood. He always stopped by their pond in the spring to serenade her and Captain Splash with his newest songs. Now that she was so lonely, it seemed worth the risk to talk to an old friend.

But Waga knew nothing of all of this. He only knew that Belle was doing the forbidden thing of entering the forest—something no self-respecting duck would ever do.

"Let her just stay in the woods among the wild things," he raged to Hannah. "I'll not have her back on this pond."

For the rest of the day Hannah sat daydreaming on her nest. She was by nature curious, if not bold, and her mind was racing with fantasies about what might have happened to Belle. She pictured her one moment being devoured by the weasel, and the next all in one piece eating woodland berries with Green Hood and his friends.

In her heart Hannah wished that she had the courage to go out into the woods and have a few adventures too. But she knew that Waga would never allow her to wander from their secure little world.

That night was an unusually glorious one. There was a full moon and it made a white path through the water like a silver carpet to swim on. Waga was snoozing on the bank of the pond. Hannah was on her nest. Suddenly she heard the rustle of wings, and saw two figures perched on the stone wall. They were talking gaily to each other. The wind carried their words to her nest.

"I'll leave you here, Belle. I don't think old Sour Berry will let me go near your willow tree."

"When will you return?" asked Belle.

"In a few weeks, I suppose. I want to try some ponds to the north. I'll circle back if I don't find the Silver Crane up there. It may have been a false rumor that he was seen heading this way."

"I wish you luck."

"And I hope Captain Splash gets out of the hospital by the time I get back."

"He will," said Belle. "I just know he will."

"Let me sing you a little song before I leave, like in the old days," said Green Hood. And his voice rose up into the silence of the night.

In search of the Silver Crane
I wait, I wait, but not in vain.
    Someday I shall hear his voice
    And in his loving wings rejoice.
    Someday I shall see his beak
    And know the answers that I seek.
Someday he will come to me.
Someday he will come to me.

In search of the Silver Crane
Long hours by each pond I've lain.
    Oh dream I carry in my breast
    Oh hope that drives me without rest
    Continually from nest to nest,
    Surely ducks who seek are blest.
Someday he will come to me.
Someday he will come to me.

In search of the Silver Crane
I take to the skies again.

 Be my journey without end,
 Still my weary way I wend,
 Ever airborne without cease
 Toward him who grants a feathered peace.
Someday he will come to me.
Someday he will come to me.

And then Belle's voice chimed in:

Someday he will come to me.
Someday he will come to me!

What marvelous voices they had. Like some heavenly choir rising to the sky. Hannah wanted to join in the singing too, to soar along with their flight. But what would Waga think if he heard her? He might not approve. And so instead she jumped off her nest and ran across the dark meadow to where he was sleeping on the bank.

"Waga, did you hear? It's Green Hood and Belle," she quacked.

"I'd be deaf if I hadn't heard," he replied grumpily, scratching the back of his head with his right foot the way he sometimes did when he was angry. "Haven't they any more sense than to wake sleeping ducks in the middle of the night?"

"Oh, Waga, I don't think they meant any harm."

"I don't care what they meant," stormed Waga. "I'll not have my rest disturbed like this. Belle is not allowed back on this pond. In the morning I will tell her so."

Hannah didn't want to hear any more. She went back to her nest without another word. Poor Belle. What would happen if Captain Splash came back and she wasn't there? How could Belle manage in the wilderness on her own? And yet, Hannah told herself, Waga usually knew what was best for everyone. She'd just have to be silent and see what happened.

And she fell into a deep, dreamless sleep.

5
Captain Splash

Waga woke the next morning with a sudden twitching of his tail. It always twitched when he was upset about something. For a moment he forgot what that something was. Then he remembered the loud singing of the night before and that he was to send Belle away. Well, he would do it right now while it was still fresh in his mind. As if to underscore his resolution, he grabbed a fish that foolishly passed under his beak and shook it violently in the air.

Waga was just about to swallow the fish when he noticed his Master approaching. He was carrying a huge creature in his arms, pressing its wings close against his body as he calmed it with soothing words. "There now, Captain Splash, everything is going to be all right. Belle is here waiting for you." Then he released the struggling bird, which Waga could see was twice the size of himself. It plunged right into the pond, splashing about, its wings stirring up great waves in the water.

Waga watched the scene in horror, the fish lodged in his throat. "Here's another friend for you, Waga," he heard his Master saying. "Belle will be happy to see he is out of the hospital."

Belle zoomed across the pond as if she had heard her name mentioned. When he saw her, Captain Splash stopped thrashing about and sped toward her, his sleek body shining in the water.

Waga trembled with fear. Never had he seen such a gigantic duck. And all black and green—not even part white like Belle. His Master had already turned back to the house, leaving him to face this newcomer alone.

Waga just sat there quaking on the shore. He knew he could not pick a quarrel with such an enormous creature. He had his unborn ducklings to think of. They would be father-less, poor things, if anything happened to him. He couldn't let that happen. No, he must be unselfish and let Captain Splash and Belle stay.

"Ahoy, Mate!" Captain Splash called to Belle as he swam toward her.

"Ahoy, Captain!" she called in response. "You're looking ship-shape again!"

"Ay, lassie, the wing's a mite stiff, but I can still splash about like the old days," he replied. And he flapped his wings out, and thrashed about a bit to prove his point.

"This ought to impress the old weasel if he's watching," he added, taking a dive below the surface and coming up on the other side of Belle.

"There's not a weasel alive who's the match for you, Captain Splash," she laughed.

"Come on, lassie, splash about a bit too and get that caked mud off your feathers," said Captain Splash. "I don't think you've fixed up since I left." And he chased her playfully out to the middle of the pond where they frolicked about like carefree ducklings.

When Hannah came back to the pond later that afternoon, she was amazed to see Belle prancing gaily about under the willow tree, drying her newly groomed feathers in the sun. Captain Splash was watching her contentedly.

"How wonderful that Captain Splash is out of the hospital," she sighed more to herself than to Waga. And after a quick swim and some cracked corn, she hurried back to her nest.

As for Waga, he breathed more freely when he realized that Belle and Captain Splash were staying on their side of the pond. They settled under the willow tree as if he weren't around. Well, he would just act as if they weren't around either. That was obviously the solution.

Waga even managed to control his anger when he saw Belle leading Captain Splash into the feeding pen. He pretended to be so busy pulling a grass root that he could not possibly notice what they were doing. They had to eat too, he told himself, as long as they were staying here. How long that would be, he didn't dare to let himself think.

"Not bad cracked corn," said Captain Splash after taking a hearty share. "Looks like we're going to have smooth sailing from now on."

"Except for old Sour Berry over there," said Belle. "He's not what I'd call jolly company."

"I can understand how he feels," said Captain Splash. "Until now he's had the place all to himself. It's hard to have two captains on one ship, you know."

"But you never minded other ducks coming on our pond."

"Well, lassie, we Muscovies can fly," said Captain Splash. "Even as ducklings we knew there was a world beyond our own. Our friend here just hasn't had a chance to learn that."

"And he doesn't want to," said Belle.

"He'll mellow up after a while," said the Captain. "You wait and see."

And then as if all this outpouring of wisdom had exhausted him, Captain Splash settled his large body down under the willow tree for a long nap.

Later that week Belle made her way to the tool shed where Hannah was setting.

"I hope you don't mind my making a nest here too," she said. "But I think I'll go *under* the shed."

"Go right ahead," said Hannah generously.

Belle made her way through a tiny opening under the floor boards and huddled in the soft earth below. "Are you safe there in the open?" she called out to Hannah. "You mentioned that weasel. It's much more protected where I am."

"Waga says the weasel never comes over the wall," replied Hannah.

"I wouldn't be so sure."

"And I like it out here, besides," added Hannah. "I can catch the breeze and even see some of the pond in the distance."

71

"As you please," said Belle. "But I wouldn't like to be so exposed."

There was silence for a time while Belle settled in. And then Hannah got up enough courage to ask Belle something she had been wondering about. "Have you ever had any ducklings before?"

"Have I had ducklings!" Belle responded with a cackle. "Why, I've had so many ducklings, I could have given half of them away and not even known they were gone!"

Belle now entered Hannah's routine of setting all day and appearing only in the late afternoons for food and water. Waga and Captain Splash were left alone on the pond. Each morning the Captain greeted Waga with

"Ahoy, Mate!", but Waga would just swim past without a reply.

With everything Waga had to think of, the weeks passed like a flight of birds before a gathering storm. And as if things weren't bad enough, Waga was startled one morning to see a mother mallard had made her way onto the pond with a line of little ones behind her. He immediately put his head down in a charging position and zoomed toward them.

"Madam," he quacked fiercely, "this is private property. Please leave."

"Oh, kind sir," said the mallard, "would you chase away a new mother?"

For a moment Waga stopped to consider this. Then he recovered his warlike stance. "I would."

"But my ducklings have just hatched in the forest. They have never seen a pond before."

"They will never see this one again."

"Please let us stay until they learn to fly."

"I'll make them fly right now if you don't go."

"But I'm so afraid for them in the forest. The weasel may get them."

"That is not my concern, Madam." And Waga chased them across the pond and over the meadow to a chink in the stone wall.

"Green Hood warned me and my husband you were a sour berry," she called back to him. "And he was right. Sour Berry! Sour Berry! I hope the weasel comes and gets you!" And with that she disappeared.

"Whew," Waga muttered to himself when she was gone. "A duck just can't waddle

quietly around in his own little pond any-
more."

And with a sigh for the good old days that
were, Waga tucked his head under his wing
and fell into a deep midmorning snooze.

6
The Weasel

Hannah came waddling down to the pond that afternoon full of news.

"I'm sure I felt a duckling stir in the third egg on the left," she quacked. "It's only a matter of days, maybe hours, before they'll hatch."

She could hardly talk of anything else between gobbles of cracked corn. And just as Waga was about to report his adventure with the mallard mother, she was suddenly rushing off.

"I really must go!" she called back. "I don't want to miss those ducklings!"

As soon as Hannah reached her nest, she counted her eggs, as she always did. One, two, three, four, five, six . . . six eggs. Only six? Where were the other three? She poked around with her beak a bit, but there were none caught up in the fine matting of leaves and feathers on which they rested.

She was too embarrassed to say anything to Belle who seemed to have found her nest in perfect order. She had once told Hannah she had ten eggs, and Hannah had never heard her change that number. It seemed better to go straight to Waga. Maybe he could make things right again.

"My dear!" she quacked, her voice shrill, her feathers all askew. "There are only six eggs in my nest instead of the usual nine!"

"Don't be silly," said Waga, more gruffly than he intended. "That's impossible."

"It's true," cried Hannah. "Only six! I counted carefully just now."

"Perhaps you counted wrong in the first place," said Waga.

"No, there were always nine before," insisted Hannah. "I'm sure of it."

"There must have been only six," said Waga. "If you turn the number nine upside down, you get six."

"Oh, *I* feel all turned upside down," cried Hannah.

"You may have a touch of sunstroke from setting on the eggs too long," said Waga.

"Now take a swim and don't worry about a thing."

"Yes, my dear," replied Hannah, doing as she was told.

But Waga couldn't help worrying about Hannah after she had returned to her nest again. Her feathers were looking frayed these days and her beak had faded to a much paler orange.

"I'll see that she takes care of herself after the ducklings are here," he told himself.

That evening Hannah was very nervous setting on her nest. Every sound, the croaking of a frog, the stirring of a muskrat, seemed to be a threat of some kind. Beyond the wall she could hear a mother rabbit scurrying by with her babies as clearly as if they were beside her. And then she heard some scratching sounds,

like a squirrel or chipmunk burrowing frantically into some new shelter.

She sat frozen with fear. And then she heard it—a new song of the forest animals. At first it was breathed only in whispers. Then it spread until it seemed the swell of the voices of all the woodland creatures rising in the wind would be enough to awaken the weasel himself, if he were asleep.

THE NEW SONG
OF THE FOREST ANIMALS

Lo, the weasel just went by,
We don't know where, we don't know why.
At first he crept, and then he ran,
As if he had some terrible plan.
Stay silent as he passes near,
Don't let your voices catch his ear.

Beware the weasel, oh beware!
The weasel wanders everywhere.

Was it possible, thought Hannah, that the weasel could have taken her three missing eggs? No, she must have counted wrong in the first place, as Waga said. There must have been only six all along.

Hannah dozed fitfully in the sun most of the next day. When it was time to go down to the pond that afternoon, Belle stopped by cheerily for her.

"Come along, ducky," she said. "I'm so thirsty, I could drink the whole pond dry."

"I think maybe I won't go down today," said Hannah shakily.

"Now don't be foolish," said Belle. "None of the eggs will hatch while you're away.

New mothers are all aflutter just about this time. But when you've had as many as I have, you just let things be."

"All right," said Hannah, getting up reluctantly. "Maybe it will do me some good to get away for a while. And I suppose Waga will be disappointed if I don't appear."

When Hannah returned to her nest after a quiet swim with Waga, she set about counting her eggs very calmly. One . . . one . . . one . . . one egg! This time she searched desperately, poking with her foot as well as her beak deep into the matting. But there was still only *one* egg. Too horrified to say anything to Belle who was already on her nest under the shed, she went tearing down to Waga.

"Waga, Waga, there is only *one* egg. I just counted and there is only one!"

Waga felt himself go limp.

"What do you mean?" was all he could manage to get out.

"There is only one egg! I counted as I do every afternoon and that's all there is."

"We must be calm about this," said Waga, although he did not feel too calm himself.

"How can we be calm?" wailed Hannah.

Waga had to think fast. "Well, if it is true that there is just one egg, perhaps it is for the best. We'll have just one duckling. That may be quite enough. He'll be easier to take care of, and he won't make as much noise as nine."

"I would be grateful for even one," said Hannah, cheering up a little at the thought of her baby duckling. "I'd better be getting back to him now." And she padded off into the dark shadows beyond the meadow.

Waga watched her disappear with shining eyes. He was proud of her, his dear, sweet, faithful Hannah. He was still having these tender thoughts when the air was pierced by the most heart-rending quack he had ever heard.

And then he saw Hannah stumbling toward him. "Waga . . . I . . . I just saw the weasel going over the wall with an egg in his mouth. And the nest is . . . empty!"

This time Waga was too stunned to reply. He just sat there staring open-beaked at Hannah.

"He's the one who's been taking my eggs. I should never have left my nest. Oh, my egg!

My duckling . . . my son!" And Hannah fell into a sobbing heap of feathers on the bank.

Belle came flying down to the pond now.

"I saw the weasel too!" she cried. "I saw his legs flash by from under the shed!"

"Ahoy, Mate, are you safe?" called Captain Splash, swimming over.

"I'm fine," replied Belle. "But, Hannah, you would have been a goner if you had been on the nest. He might have gotten you."

"I wish he had," moaned Hannah. "I wish he had!"

"Are you sure your eggs are out of his reach?" asked Captain Splash.

"Oh, that sneaky thief could never get through the small hole I have under the shed," said Belle confidently. But she flew quickly back to her nest anyway.

Waga and Hannah were left alone on the bank. Waga did what he could to comfort her —a gentle peck here and there, a little fanning with his wings—but Hannah quacked pathetically for hours. Finally she fell into deep slumber next to her rock.

Waga did not sleep all night. He had put his dreams into his sons—and then his son. Now there would be no one. Not even a daughter to comfort him in his old age. Already he felt old. So much had happened this past month, and now this. Why to him, when all he had been trying to do was mind his own business?

Well, somehow he must bear it, he told himself, although he knew it was unbearable. He and Hannah had lived alone without ducklings until now, and so they would have to live from now on.

He gazed now and then out into the pond, but saw nothing—not even the mallard mother who was swimming nervously with her little ones on the other side.

7
The Visit

The next morning Hannah was strangely silent, just staring into space.

"You must eat something," Waga told her. "Shall I bring you a little goldfish?"

Hannah did not answer. She just huddled closer against the large rock she loved so much, as if it were an enchanted egg that might magically hatch forth her lost ducklings.

Waga was hoping that Hannah would soon

be her old self again. For a few days he waited patiently, coaxing her, fussing over her, trying to serve her. But she seemed not to see or hear him, as if she were in a world of her own.

The pond was unusually quiet these days. Belle and Captain Splash kept to themselves in the late afternoons. They did not want to disturb Hannah. Even the mallard mother seemed to know that this was a special time and stayed away with her ducklings.

"Wouldn't you like to take a little swim?" Waga would ask Hannah every few hours. But she would merely shake her head and stay where she was. Her body looked like a wilted feathered cushion that had been washed up on the bank.

"A tiny piece of cracked corn?"

Once he thought he saw a spark of interest

in her eyes. But then it would fade out again, like a flame with nothing to nourish it.

By the end of one week Waga was worried. By the next he was desperate. A duck has to eat. What could he do? Hannah would die of a broken heart or starvation if she kept on like this. And what would he do without her?

That night, sitting miserably at her side, he looked up into the dark sky and came as close as a duck could to prayer. He was in a kind of fever himself, neither able to sleep nor stay awake. The moon was hidden behind veils of mist. Her rays played dimly on the pond, giving it a faint unearthly glow.

Waga felt his mind becoming as hazy as the scene about him. "Oh, someone help me!" he moaned aloud. "I need help!" He would doze off for a few moments and then be abruptly awake again. In both states he could hear his own pitiful cry: "Help! Help!"

And then—was it possible?—he thought he saw a silver form out on the water. It stayed still in one spot as if it were rooted there. Its long neck curved as gracefully as a tall reed. Its wings were folded into its body like the petals of a water lily.

It couldn't be! And yet it was—a crane. The Silver Crane!

Waga realized that he was the only one who could see the visitor at that moment. Hannah was asleep, her head buried under her wing in such a way as to shut herself off from everything. Captain Splash was cradled as usual in his own feathered darkness under the willow tree. It was as if here in the misty night Waga and the Silver Crane were the only two birds on earth.

What should he do? What was a duck supposed to do when he came upon the Silver Crane? He tried to recall what Green Hood had told him. He could remember nothing. If only he had listened carefully. But at that time he had not been interested.

Waga watched as the Silver Crane slowly bent its head as if listening to the light breathing of the creatures below. And then it looked forward, directly at him. Its cool, silvery eyes seemed to see right through him. And yet there was something loving in their gaze. Something that made Waga feel warm and safe.

Without knowing what he was doing, Waga swam out from shore toward the Silver

Crane. But he dared not go too close. He wondered if the Silver Crane would speak first. Or should he? He felt suddenly small and humble. And then he heard his voice crying out: "Oh, Silver Crane, what am I to do? Don't let Hannah die!"

A torrent of words flowed from Waga's beak—things he had never told anyone. Things he didn't even understand about himself until now.

"I know I've been mean and selfish all my life," he told the Silver Crane, "but I didn't want to be. I didn't know how to act differently. I'll do anything you say if you'll only tell me how to save Hannah. Tell me where the answer is to be found!"

Then the Silver Crane spoke. Its voice was like water rippling onto rocks through narrow mountain ravines.

"There is no place on earth where the answer is not," it said.

"But tell me *exactly* where," pleaded Waga. "I only know my own little pond."

"Right here in the water of your pond," said the Silver Crane. "In the grass that grows in your meadow. In the trees that stand watch over you."

"I don't understand," cried Waga.

"In yourself."

"In myself? Oh, can't you say it more clearly?" implored Waga. "I still don't understand."

The Silver Crane paused for a moment. And then it said, "You must let things be."

"Let things be?"

"Inside and outside are the same," said the Silver Crane. "Large and small, light and dark, black and white, they are all the same."

"But how can that be?" cried Waga.

"The same," repeated the Silver Crane. And with these last words the Silver Crane began fading away from him. Was it the hum of the cicadas in the distance or did he hear the Silver Crane's song farther and farther off:

> *Be it day or be it night*
> *White is black, and black is white.*
> *Inside, outside are the same*
> *Though we give a different name.*
> *What things are we may not see,*
> *But we must let all things be.*

"Oh, don't go! Don't leave me, Silver Crane!" cried Waga. "You still haven't told me what to do."

"Let things be," said the Silver Crane. Its voice sounded so far away now it seemed like a tiny drop of water trickling onto a single stone. "Let things be."

And the Silver Crane was gone. Just a puff of silver mist hung over the water where it had been.

Waga swam back to shore as if in a trance. He felt light and joyous inside. The Silver Crane had somehow lifted a great weight from him, leaving him relaxed and free.

"I shall let things be," he told himself, tucking his head under his wing for a long deserved sleep. But he couldn't help adding wistfully, "Whatever that means."

8
The Tenth Duckling

Waga opened his eyes at dawn. Even with his few hours sleep, he felt refreshed, as if reborn. He glanced quickly over at Hannah to see if she would notice that something about him had changed. But she wasn't looking at him. She continued to gaze down with sad, empty eyes.

"She may be too weak to recognize the difference in me," he told himself. Then he plunged into the water and swam deliberately past Captain Splash to see if he would notice. But the Captain was busy fishing and let him sail by without even his usual "Ahoy, Mate."

However, perhaps he really was different because when he saw the mallard mother stealing with her ducklings onto the pond, he didn't chase them. Her husband was there too this time, but he just let them be, as if it were perfectly natural to have them there.

When Waga returned to Hannah on the bank, he was astonished to find her standing up, her eyes bright with excitement.

"She's noticed my change after all," he said to himself.

But no, she was staring out across the meadow toward the tool shed. There was Belle marching down the lawn to the pond with ten little ducklings prancing single file after her—each one no more than a yellow spot of fluff with tiny brown markings on it.

Captain Splash stopped where he was, a fish still wriggling in his beak. He let the fish drop as he called: "Ahoy, Mates!"

Belle strutted proudly to the water's edge and stepped carefully into it. And then, marvel of all marvels, the ten little yellow spots slid into the water and followed their mother in neat formation across the pond toward their father.

That is, all except the tenth duckling. This silly creature just couldn't keep in line, and kept wandering off too far from one side or the other. He was so confused that sometimes he just fluttered about in circles.

"Isn't he adorable!" quacked Hannah, her

first words in days. And she leapt into the water after the tenth duckling. She swam just in front of him and managed to lead him back to his place at the end of the line.

Waga trailed hesitantly after her. "Careful now," he cautioned Hannah. "Don't tire yourself."

"I'm fine!" quacked Hannah gaily, motioning him away with a flap of her wing. And she continued guiding the tenth duckling who could not seem to keep his place without her.

Waga did not want to argue with her, especially since he was so happy to see her active again. So he just let her be, a member of Belle's colorful family.

All morning the ducklings paraded back and forth through the water after their mother, with Hannah bringing up the rear. About noon they collapsed on top of each other in a brown and yellow heap under the willow tree. Hannah left them for the first time to race over to Waga.

"Waga! Waga!" she quacked.

"Yes?"

"Waga, isn't it wonderful! Our duckling, our son, is here at last!"

"What do you mean, Hannah?" was all he could manage to say.

"The tenth one in line is *our* duckling!" she cried.

"But how can that be?" asked Waga.

"Well," replied Hannah breathlessly, "Belle should have had only nine eggs like I did. It's only fair. But she has *ten* ducklings. And since I am missing my last egg, surely her tenth duckling is mine."

Waga was speechless from the madness of Hannah's logic. She had never been a clear thinker before, but this was the most muddled he had ever heard her.

"My dear Hannah," he said, trying to reason with her a bit. "The last duckling could not possibly be ours. He is not all yellow as ours would have been. He has brown spots. That means he won't be pure white when he grows up."

"I don't care!" cried Hannah. "Yellow and brown, white and black, they're all the same to me!"

The way she said it sent a chill through Waga. She sounded like the Silver Crane. Is this what he had meant, what Hannah was saying now? How wise she suddenly seemed. For a moment he thought she must be right.

"And he's about the same age our duckling

would have been," she added to support her argument. "So he must be ours."

"But remember he comes from someone else's egg," cautioned Waga slowly. "He won't look or act like us when he grows up. He'll be different from us."

"A duckling should be different when he grows up . . . no matter whose egg he comes from," said Hannah with finality. "He has to be himself." And that ended the discussion for a moment.

But then Hannah whispered softly, "Oh, Waga, say he can be our own little duckling, our very own."

"He can be," said Waga gently, and he felt his heart pounding with joy. But he added quickly, "That is, if Belle agrees to it. She may not want to give him up."

Hannah went scurrying out to Belle faster than Waga had ever seen her move, even in her youngest, most active days. He never knew the words that passed between them, but he saw Belle zigging and zagging with her brood in such a way that the last duckling could not follow. And he felt his heart pounding as Hannah guided that tenth duckling away from the others, toward him on the bank.

"My duckling, my son!" cried Waga, without realizing what he was going to say. He puffed his white chest out with pride. How good it was to have a son of his own. He was so busy planning all the things he would teach him to do, he didn't even notice the wild mallard mother and her husband swimming right past with their ducklings, until they were practically on top of him. There were eleven yellow and brown babies in all, and except for their larger size, they looked incredibly like his own.

"How lovely they are," Hannah called to the mother, who was nervously watching Sour Berry out of the corner of her eye. But Hannah, unaware of anything except her own happiness, continued, "They'll be such nice friends for our son while he is growing up. What fun they'll have together." And turning to Waga, she added, "He'll need lots of playmates, won't he, since he is an only duckling?"

"I suppose they can teach him things I don't know," said Waga thoughtfully. "After all, they are different from us. They are wild."

"And yet they are the same," said Hannah. Again she sounded like the Silver Crane.

"Yes, the same," agreed Waga, a slight chill going through his body.

"Be sure they get enough to eat," Hannah told the mallard mother. "Take them into the feeding pen. There's plenty for all."

The mallard mother was certain this would send Waga into his usual flap, but he just nodded his head pleasantly in agreement.

"Something strange has happened on this pond," she whispered to her husband.

9
Duckling Day

That afternoon a dark speck appeared in the sky and gradually became larger until it was hovering right over the pond. Then it came in for a landing, its wings held stiffly like an airplane, until its feet touched the water. It was Green Hood.

"Snails and quails, how gay! It looks like duckling day!" he called cheerily.

"It is!" quacked Hannah. "Come and join us!"

"Ducklings here, ducklings there, ducklings, ducklings everywhere!" exclaimed Green Hood, swimming over.

He glided playfully past the mallard babies, greeting their parents. He was careful not to show surprise at seeing them there.

And then he noticed the nine newborn Muscovies. "Ahoy, Mate," he called merrily to Captain Splash. "So you've joined the ship again."

"Never left it, Mate," said Captain Splash. "Just went below for a spell."

"You've a fine crew there," said Green Hood to Belle.

And then glancing over at the tiny duckling huddled next to Waga, he exclaimed, "I see that you have a fine lad there too. This calls for a celebration! I shall compose a song for all the ducklings."

And he sang in a full, melodious voice:

THE DUCKLING SONG

Hey ding a ding, to ducklings I sing,
Little ducklings all in a row.
With a cheep, cheep, a hop and leap,
Into this world they go.

Hey ding a dong, summer is long,
And a pond is a perfect place
To swim and play, to fish all day,
And have a duckling race.

Hey ding a ho, soon you shall know
The lakes and rivers and sea.
Soon you shall fly into the sky
And round the world with me.

116

Hey ding a dell, mark my words well,
Youth is the time to be king.
Soon you shall be grown up like me—
Mere ducks without a ling.

"Oh, it's too wonderful!" quacked Hannah when he was finished.

"Your best yet, Mate," said Captain Splash, while Belle nodded her head in agreement.

Even the ducklings seemed to know that it was special, for they all started cheeping merrily during the song.

"All's well that hatches well," said Green Hood.

"Ay, laddie, except that the weasel is still around," said Captain Splash.

A moment's hush fell over them, like the cloud's shadow passing over the sun.

117

"There will always be weasels," said Green Hood solemnly. And then the lilt returned to his voice. "Just as there will always be the Silver Crane."

"Did you find him on this last trip?" asked Belle.

Again the hush.

"No, I didn't," Green Hood replied at last. "There was no sign of him anywhere—not a ripple on the water, not a crackling of a twig, not a shimmer in the air to make one feel he was anywhere near."

"Maybe you should give up," suggested Hannah. "You like this pond so much. You could just settle down permanently on our cracked corn and fish."

"Never," said Green Hood dreamily. "I am a true poet of the skies. I'll just stay long enough to do a little moulting and get my flying feathers in shape. Then I'll be off again after the Silver Crane. I'm sure he must be somewhere just beyond."

"Oh, I'm sure too," said Hannah, perching up on her favorite rock, which seemed to glow with the same happiness as her own. "You deserve to see him after all this time."

"Perhaps you've already seen him," said Waga mysteriously.

"Snails and quails, what do you mean?" asked Green Hood.

"I mean maybe you've all seen him here and there, now and then, but you haven't been aware of it," replied Waga. "He was so much a part of you that he didn't have to make a special appearance. It was just me who hadn't known what he was like . . . until now."

Everyone turned to Waga in amazement to find out what he meant. But he merely shoved off into the water.

"Where are you going?" they called.

"For a long, relaxed swim on the pond," he replied gaily. "I need time to think about my new duckling and all that's happened."

"Come back!" they quacked impatiently. "We want to hear more."

"Then listen to the grass in the meadow, the leaves on the trees," said Waga. "Let things be."

And he suddenly seemed quite different to those who watched him from the shore. His soft white body was no longer puffed up haughtily. It floated on the water with an air of wise calm. And his eyes had a faraway look that not even Hannah had ever noticed in them before. As if he had seen some rare and fabled land. He seemed at peace with the world. As if he were another duck.

"What's happened?" they called.

"Let things be," he merely repeated as he drifted farther and farther away. "Let things be."

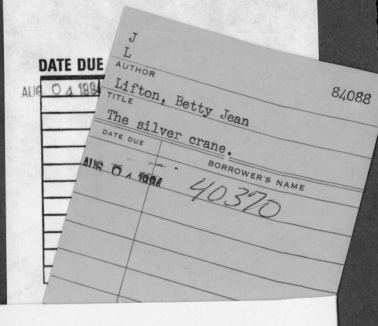